Angels
on
Earth

Steven
LUNDQUIST

Printed in the United States of America

ISBN 979-8-89114-235-0 (sc)
ISBN 979-8-89114-236-7 (e)

Library of Congress Control Number: 2025922953

2026.01.12

MainSpring Books
5901 W. Century Blvd
Suite 750
Los Angeles, CA, US, 90045

www.mainspringbooks.com

Contents

Synopsis

<u>The Haunting</u>:

A hard ride into Bucharest in 1890. The Count's most powerful warrior has been ordered to find and rescue the Count's bride-to-be, as well as to retrieve the powerful love potion that was created for the two lovers to consume at their wedding. This is a Tristan and Isolde type of story where the wrong two lovers drink the potion by mistake, and then are forced to deal with the extreme consequences that most certainly will ensue.

<u>Bonnie's Dream</u>:

A young lady of nineteen comes of age in her hometown of West Dallas during the early stages of the great depression in 1930. Unfortunately, she's developing a rather severe drinking problem which causes her dreams about the infamous gangsters of her time to become real in her life. This story is a rather unusual take on an actual person who lived during the heyday of notorious gangsters in the deep south of the 1930s.

<u>The Spanish Steps</u>:

A grieving husband in the heart of Rome, out for a brief stroll to test his badly injured legs, suddenly finds himself alone at the bottom of The Spanish Steps. Against all reason, he decides to climb the steps under the most difficult of circumstances. A walk becomes a crawl when he has to call on every ounce of his courage to accomplish his goal.

<u>Angels of Ushuaia</u>:

In the old west of the 1870's, a famous lawman is cut down by a bullet to the back of his skull. Thus begins a wild journey that takes him to the ends of the earth while searching for a killer; a search that ends in the southernmost city in the world. Is he still alive? Is he heading toward hell? Has he already arrived? A most unusual group of angels comes into his life to help facilitate his arrival; be it to heaven or hell, he's not sure.

<u>The Visitors</u>:

A lonely angel, living high above the earth, decides to rebel against God's commands and seek out a bride from among the human population. His overwhelming need for the love of a beautiful woman puts him squarely at odds with the natural laws of Heaven; for an angel and a human can never be allowed to join together in marriage. God has never allowed an exception to his natural laws, so the dilemma for the lonely angel will have to be resolved in a most frightening and fatal determination.

The Haunting

The streets of despair; a rainy afternoon in Bucharest in 1890. Leaves strewn about like toy candy, waiting to be devoured in a frenzy by starving street urchins scanning the stones for locks of abundance; beggars on the street listening warily for sounds of engagement from the foreign intruders; brutality unfurled upon the meek; rivers of treachery flowing beneath the bricks.

An emaciated young woman, huddling in the corner of a collapsed building, awakens to a battalion of Clydesdales battling through the cobblestones. A group of riders in battle armour have descended from seemingly far beyond the heavens. The leader, a bold, striking man, suddenly cries out, "Anna!" The others quickly follow his lead, "Anna!" "Anna!" "Anna!" "Anna!" The cry goes out twentyfold.

The mysterious Count intends for her to be his bride. He was stunned by her gaunt loveliness on a recent trip through the city in the dead of night. She had been walking barefoot in the street as his golden, horse-drawn carriage passed by. Her inherent beauty was beyond anything he had ever imagined.

The Count's attendants were instructed to call out to her, but for some reason they couldn't reach her. She seemed to be lost. When the Count looked back for her she was gone. He demanded to know her name from the mob surrounding his carriage.

"What's her name? Get it for me!"

The Count was told that someone in the mob had heard her being called Anna by another man on the street. The Count was not happy that another man had been calling out to her while his carriage passed by. He wanted her for his own. He wanted her love.

"Where is she?" demanded the Count.

Over the next several nights, the Count realized that he had become intoxicated with unrelenting lust for this alluring young temptress. He needed her love. He had to have it. In his despair, he instructed his court magicians to concoct the most powerful love potion known to mankind: a shrouded, guarded recipe enhanced with rose petals, essence of lavender, pine bark extract, and pure oil of sandalwood.

The desire for intimacy becomes overwhelming if two participants are willing to drink from this potion while kneeling next to each other in prayer; for only God can know the true secret of love.

While holding hands in prayer, two innocents have been known to fall deeply and inconceivably in love with each other for extended periods of time, sometimes throughout the rest of their lives.

When the potion had been concocted, the Count ordered a group of twenty of his warriors to ride back to the city to find this somewhat undernourished young maiden and bring her back to his quarters for a feast and celebration. His demands were to find her quickly, then force her to ride back with them, even if they had to bolt her to the saddle.

If anyone or any group tried to object, the Count's orders were simply to have them arrested and incarcerated on the spot. No questions asked. No answers given. The warriors were then to ride to the magicians' quarters to procure and tightly secure the love potion that the Count intended to give to his budding bride. This location was approximately an hour's ride from their final destination.

The Count realized that only his prime warrior could be trusted to complete this task without incident: a warrior whose loyalty to the Count was unswerving; whose abilities had been tested through a multitude of broken backs, butchered shields, and shredded body armour. The all-powerful Tristan had never been defeated in battle, even against insurmountable odds.

But one of Tristan's subordinates was convinced that this unlikely endeavor would be all for naught. A woman of dubious background plucked right off the street, with nothing but sheer, natural beauty for a dowry? Beauty compromised by ill-fitting clothes, spurious hygiene, a dearth of manners, limited education, and who knows what else? Would the Count really choose such a commoner for a bride? A rank plebeian? For a concubine, perhaps, but for a bride?

"Look … You were all out here with me the other night when we were riding with the Count. We all saw her walking in the street. Kind of a pretty face, right? Well, let's call it like it is: She's a pathetic looking bitch. Sunken cheeks, undernourished, very little meat on her bones.

"Why in the world would this man, if he's really a man, why would he want her for a bride? He'll be sick of her before they even get through their wedding night. After we find her I'm going to drag her out behind one of those rat trap huts that line the back streets. We'll get one of the newbies to gouge off her stinking street rags, and then we can all just settle in and have a little fun.

"What are there, twenty of us? Hell, if we keep it moving, we should all be able to get in a few nice, deep, juicy pokes, as long as she doesn't die on us right away. When we're through with her, we'll just toss her sickening body into one of those fire pits out in the back. We can watch her burn for an hour or two and then we'll just tell the Count she couldn't be found. We tried. She just disappeared."

"Are you talking about Anna?"

"Tristan, I'm sorry. I didn't mean anything by it. I was just thinking out loud. You know I would never do anything against the Count."

But the edge of Tristan's sword had already penetrated the unfortunate warrior's throat for up to two inches, causing him to cough and vomit vociferously. His companions watched in horror as he attempted to beg for his final breath, but the shaft of Tristan's raw, searing blade was slowly and deliberately forcing its way through his collapsing neck and up through the base of his skull.

"Leave him! He stays on his horse while he dies. Two or three of you grab some firewood and bolt it to his back like a cross. I want him sitting straight up in his saddle. He's a warrior, after all. We'll leave him right where he is so all these people on the street can gawk at him. They're going to have to learn that we have no intention of taking prisoners. They're just going to have to give her up."

Tristan called out to the crowd. "Greetings from the Count's most powerful warriors. We've come to retrieve the Count's new bride and remove her from the street. Her name might be 'Anna.' If anybody knows where 'Anna' is, or anything about her, tell us now. Your life may depend on it."

Then quietly turning to his warriors: "All right, get him up on his cross while the rest of you take a deep breath and go out and find her. Be kind to these people. We don't want to have to put down a riot. But find her! No excuses!"

He turned back and shouted to the crowd. "One more blessing from the Count of Transylvania. For anyone who brings Anna to me quickly, the Count has instructed me to reward you with fifty Romanian Leu along with ten loaves of fresh bread and any other delicacies you can get your hands on. Bring Anna to me now, alive and in good health, and the gift is yours."

The crowd began to chant. "Anna!" "Anna!" "Anna!" "Anna!"

Within moments, something or someone was spotted high up on the roof of the Russian Orthodox church across the street. The crowd shuddered and pointed to the roof en masse. Something was hovering motionless near the very edge of the steeple, staring down at the crowd.

"I think that's her up on the steeple! How did she get up there? She's not moving!"

"Wait a minute. There ain't no stairs all the way up to the roof. I know that church. There's a bell tower around toward the back."

"You're all fools. Can't you see … she's got wings."

"She ain't got no wings. Get a grip, for Christ's sake. She used the bell tower."

Tristan and the other warriors were frozen in place, staring intently up at the roof, trying to discover exactly what they thought they were seeing.

It can't be wings, thought Tristan. It can't be wings. All those stories about the Count and his lovers. The blood. The Evil. It's all been disproven. There's no way she's one of them. They don't exist!

He shook his head violently from side to side. I'm not going to listen to it. I'm not going to see it. Humans don't fly. Humans don't have wings. But how the hell did she get up there? The bell tower? She'd never make it. Never! It's way too difficult for someone that frail.

At that exact moment, a faded apparition of a beautiful young lady in the form of a butterfly gently swept down from the steeple onto the street, fluttering in place next to Tristan, smiling deep into his eyes, then quickly soaring off into the dark clouds above the city.

What the hell was that? thought Tristan. What the hell? Don't tell me that's the same person I saw walking next to our coach the other night. She was so frail she could hardly walk. How did she get down here so quickly? And why the beautiful smile? Was she flirting with me? Where the hell is she? The Count's expecting me to get her back to him quickly.

A slew of bleak, unkempt street merchants suddenly came barreling up to him, yelling and screaming. They wanted the money. "How are we expected to get her to you now? She's got wings. She flew down here like a butterfly."

"Nay, it was more like a bat," surmised one of the vendors.

"It was more like a butterfly," said another. "If she can fly away like that, how do you expect us to collect on your generous offer from the Count?"

"I don't know," stammered Tristan as he glared at the crowd. For some reason he felt himself truly starting to hate them. "I don't know anything. Just go about your business. I'll find her, then I'll make a big, fat announcement. Believe me, we're not going back to the Count without her."

"But you promised us money!"

"Then go out and get her! Bring her back to me. Just don't hurt her. If anything happens to her, you'll pay a terrible price. Do you understand me? All right, go find her and bring her to me."

The whole block of the city immediately seemed to go berserk: turning over flower carts, crawling under food wagons, running around behind buildings, accusing each other of hiding her in their clothing; nobody could see her, nobody could hear her; yet within a few frenzied moments someone had already found her and thrown her onto the street in front of Tristan.

She looked like a wounded, human butterfly, with those enticing, full-scale transparent wings that were trying so hard to flutter in the breeze. She was lying on her back, surrounded by an aggressive mob of angry street vendors, all shouting for their money. Nobody seemed to notice that this frail little thing didn't even seem to be human.

"Where did you find this butterfly?" asked Tristan.

"She ain't no butterfly," said one of the men in the street. "Give me my money. I'm the one who grabbed her and threw her on the street."

"So, where was she when you grabbed her?"

"She was hiding under my wagon. She was too weak to resist much. I think she's hungry."

"Did you hurt her in any way?"

"I had to get a little rough with her. She grabbed hold of one of the spokes on the wheel. I couldn't get a hold of her hand, so I started to pull off one of her wings; but damned if it didn't grow right back."

"Are you all right?" whispered Tristan to the frightened little creature. She seemed to be scared to death; but, oh so gentle. Is this what love looks like? thought Tristan. I can't believe I'm feeling this way. "Is your name Anna?"

"I guess it is," she replied in a faint, clear voice. "That's what they call me."

Tristan turned toward the crowd. "All right, let's get this over with. Did anyone else see her hiding under the wagon?"

"I'm the one who found her," argued another man. "I spotted her. He just pulled her out before I could grab her." But Tristan proclaimed to the crowd that fifty Romanian Leu plus ten loaves of bread would only be given to the man who actually pulled her out from under the wagon and brought her to him.

In an unusual gesture of generosity, he promised an extra five loaves of fresh bread to the man who disputed the claim, but this second man was furious that he didn't get any of the money. He began to yell profanely at Tristan, who put a stop to it immediately.

"All right, put a lid on it. I'll bring out the chains and have you beaten within an inch of your life. That's after we staple your scheming lips together. I don't expect to be back in this godforsaken town anytime soon, unless the Count demands it, so we'll just let you rot in jail until I get back."

This quickly stopped the dispute, as the people on the street all knew that Tristan was someone you didn't fool with. The reward was given out quickly, and Tristan and his frail, young companion began their journey back to another world; first to the magicians' quarters and then on to the eerie castle up on the hill.

The young lady appeared much too weak to attempt to fly away or even to ride a horse by herself, so Tristan held her in his arms as he and his band of warriors started their long journey back to the darkest place on earth. After half a day's ride they found themselves near the entrance to the magicians' quarters, spread out in a bright display of quaint, mystical huts lodged in a rich, verdant valley of great beauty.

Tristan left his frail, human-sized butterfly securely tied to the saddle of his magnificent Clydesdale while he entered the hallway to a mesmerizing array of healing textures inside the magicians' quarters. The love potion had been captured in a small vial which he found resting on a large clear quartz table laced with amethyst and pure gold.

By the time he got back to his stallion his young passenger appeared to be dying of thirst. Her eyes had glazed over and were rolling back in her head. Tristan didn't intend to unleash even a portion of this valuable concoction, but he had to do something quickly; so he cut the bolt to the top of the vial and placed the edge of the glowing, steaming love liquid to her lips.

She took her first sip while he held her in his arms. She looked at him with amazement, as if her eyes were open for the very first time. What is this feeling inside of me, she wondered? The whole world is open to me. I see the joy of existence in his eyes. My reason for living.

"Will you please take a sip with me?" she asked him so gently. "I need to feel you close to me."

Tristan was taken aback with this unusual request. The love potion was made for a special occasion. A royal wedding. It wasn't his position to interfere with the Count's commands.

"Please," she asked him again. "Just a taste. It means so much to me. For you just to take a taste with me. That way I'll know you're okay too."

"All right, little butterfly. This isn't what I intended, but if it makes you feel better … why not?"

Tristan put the vial to his lips and took a long, luxuriant taste before handing the vial back to the frail young lady. She took a longer sip this time. For a few minutes they looked into each other's eyes as they realized that their lives would never be the same.

"Tristan, my magnificent warrior, I'm not sure of this, but I think I'm falling in love with you. I think I love you even more than life, even more than death. What is this potion that we drink from? Does it show us the reason for our existence? Is it the reason why we breathe, why we cry? Does it come from a place where we die?

"I have to follow you now, my love, but you know that, don't you. I have to find your God, as you must have done before me. Even for a creature of eternal death, there must be a God. I'll fly with you in my heart, my heavenly warrior, for the rest of eternity. For there are two of us now."

Tristan was deeply overwhelmed by her expression of love, but also deeply disturbed with the depth of mistrust that he had displayed to the Count. I can't get caught up in this, he thought. It's not my place to fall in love with the Count's bride.

And yet he found that he was falling deeply and passionately in love with this human butterfly; with her long shapely legs; her beautiful wings that ran from her shoulders down to her waist; and, more than anything, her beautiful loving soul that had suddenly become attached to his soul.

As he held her in his arms, he leaned over and tenderly brushed her briefly on the forehead before lingering over her lips for several seconds. He had never before experienced a sizzling vibration of fire on his lips. He had never before known the thrill of being in love. It was more painful than any wound he had ever had to care for, overwhelming his very existence.

Tristan had been abandoned by his parents in the Romanian forest when he was not quite two years old. It was discovered later that his parents had actually been massacred by a pack of wolves; but, for some reason, the wolves had spared Tristan. He was found wandering in the wilderness and quickly carried up to the castle by the Count's attendants.

As an adult he remembered virtually nothing of his youth, only the lingering memories of being left alone in the forest. As he developed, he became fiercely strong-willed and overwhelmingly stubborn. He would acquiesce to no one but the Count.

The powerful Tristan was known to have never offered even an ounce of kindness to any of his fellow warriors. They obeyed him simply out of fear: fear of his extreme skill as a warrior, along with his powerful body and bleak determination. But mostly they feared him because of the intense darkness of his protector high up on the hill, the Count of Transylvania.

Tristan realized, as he approached the castle, that from this moment on, he would be completely vulnerable to his enemies, especially the eighteen warriors now riding alongside him. They all despised him, and they all had observed his awkward attempts at lovemaking with the Count's bride-to-be. This alone would be more than enough to unleash unspeakable torture and certain death upon any man, even for the Count's prime warrior.

The castle was now just up ahead. Tristan was numb with regret as he rehearsed his next steps. When he reached the castle he would carry the little human butterfly up the long staircase inside the castle until he reached a lift that was built strictly for visitors. The Count had never used the lift; neither had he ever been seen climbing the stairs. He was always just where he needed to be.

The love potion would accompany them up on the lift. There was enough liquid left in the vial to subdue any suspicions of deceit, but what do I say to the Count when he asks about the potion? And what do I do with her? My God, what do I do with her? How can I hand her over to him when my heart is pounding with my love for her?

As they arrived at the castle the human butterfly quietly slipped out of his arms and fluttered down to the ground, laying her head against the soft, green hillside. "My God, whoever you are, wherever you are, protect my beautiful Tristan. He doesn't know what he's in for when he steps inside the castle, but I do. Don't let me lose him forever, my God. Please keep him safe for me."

Tristan reached out for her hand, and they began to walk together into the dark, gloomy interior of the dreaded castle. The Count could never be seen during daylight hours as he suffered from a severe infection in his eyes. The light was blinding. He was only able to interact with people in the dead of night.

It was almost dark. The Count would be there soon. Tristan was prepared to hand the love vial to the Count. He released the frail little butterfly's hand and encouraged her to stand next to him.

They felt a slight, trembling breeze as they turned to see the Count standing quietly in the corner. It was now pitch dark except for the light from two large candles.

"You must be hungry, my bride! Are you ready to eat? I've prepared a spectacular feast for you! Tristan, you may join us if you wish. Go outside and dismiss your brave warriors. I discern that you're a little short-handed. One of your warriors must have stumbled and hurt himself before you returned. Where is he?"

"He doesn't feel quite himself. I believe he developed a severe headache while in Bucharest."

"It must have been something he ate. Perhaps the blade of your sword?"

"Perhaps."

"You have a propensity for handling things most efficiently, Tristan. Do you have the love potion?"

"Yes, Count."

"Keep it. I won't need it."

"But … why …?"

"I recognized her that night in the city. We've already lived through several lifetimes together. She's averse to me. Ask her. She finds no joy in knowing that she was created from my sperm."

"But … what are you trying to …?"

"I raped her mother. It's unfortunate that she takes after her mother. I've raped her hundreds of times in my mind since you've been gone. She always resists heartily, so I have to put her to sleep. I put all my victims to sleep. I'll have to rape her again tonight, no matter how much potion she drinks.

"You look confused, poor Tristan. Is this too much information for you? What are all these creatures with wings? What good are they? Why is she so weak? Have you ever asked her?"

"My mother is an angel of God."

"Her mother is the daughter of God; an archangel of the highest order. Her mother actually lived in the time of Christ. She knew him. Can you imagine that? She's unassailable. She can't be turned."

"But … I've always refused to believe that you're …"

"You're such a simple, little man, Tristan. Why are you so afraid to see what's always been right in front of you? Tell him, my bride. Tell him why you're so helpless. Tell him!"

"I drink blood, Tristan. It's the only thing I can consume. I need to drink blood. I can't live without it. I can't keep regular food in my stomach. That's why you saw me walking the streets that night in the city. I've never deliberately hurt a human, but I'm barely able to find enough sustenance from rats on the street to allow me to walk, let alone to fly."

"I intend to make love to you throughout our wedding night, my bride. You'll be very satisfied; very, very satisfied. I know that you were able to drink the love potion. Maybe that'll relax you a little. Unfortunately, Tristan attempted to deceive me by drinking it too. For that, he'll pay with his life.

"I've watched you carefully, Tristan. You've never been known to be particularly religious, and yet I've watched you from afar, on the battlefield, on your knees, praying to the son of God. How foolish you've been. You've refused to believe that your real Master is a creature of eternal death, and yet I've given you so many signs. Now, we'll find out if your God can protect you."

The count clapped his hands together several times. A small battalion of warriors began to appear outside at the entrance, all in full battle gear.

"I haven't eaten for so long," exclaimed the human butterfly. "I'm getting hungry. I'm ready now for the feast you've promised me."

She reached up and took Tristan's hand in hers, then quietly turned to face the growing throng of warriors gathering for battle at the entrance; battle with the one man who was now the true love of her existence. Her eyes suddenly glazed over with a fierce intensity. They had earlier seemed to Tristan to be a sunny, bright green, but now they had evolved into a hauntingly dark, blood red. A hissing sound emerged from between her teeth.

As the leader of the group moved aggressively toward Tristan, the human butterfly flew onto the bridge of his nose; her teeth clamped tightly between his bulging eyes. He screamed with an ungodly roar, shaking his head vigorously, trying with all his might to release her grip.

After a few moments she crawled slightly upward to entrench his forehead, from which blood began to trickle like a looming, scarlet waterfall. The warriors froze in abject fear as they realized that, within an instant, the blood had been entirely drained from this unfortunate warrior's body, which was now shriveled in a heap on the rocks in front of them.

"How weak they are, my lovely bride! This is the feast I promised you. Seventeen more souls standing right in front of you. Finish them off, my bride. Taste the blood of life. Make me proud on our wedding night. You might even find the strength to rape me!"

"I can't do this for long, my love," whispered the little butterfly to Tristan. "It would turn me forever into one of his creatures of the night. That's what he wants."

"Please, my Count," begged Tristan, "please be reasonable. These are all highly trained warriors. I've trained most of them myself. There's no need to sacrifice any more of them; no one here has betrayed you. You raised me from a little boy. Haven't I always served you with esteem? I'm asking you now to offer me the loving hand of your daughter; for the two of us to continue to honor you, perhaps with a child of our own."

"Your sense of insanity knows no bounds, Tristan. There's no future for you. You're about to die. All of you are about to die; unless, of course, my new bride decides to turn a few of you."

Tristan quickly withdrew his sword from its sheath, thrusting it deep into the Count's skull.

"Then I'm taking you with me. You'll never walk out of here alive. Neither will your treacherous soul ever fly out of here alive; if you even have a soul. You should know me by now, Count. You should know that I'd never do this for myself, but only to protect the one I love."

"That damn potion again. You ignorant fool. Don't you realize that love is just a dream for those who live in a world of eternal death; that fornication is our only rule of law? A brutal loneliness awaits me without my bride. I must have her with me! Tonight!"

The Count calmly removed the sword from his own scalp and signaled his warriors to move forward to hasten the destruction of their prime warrior. Outnumbering Tristan by a hundred to one, they pulled him down and began to beat him mercilessly.

The beautiful Anna, with her green eyes now in deep despair, fluttered in circles above them, praying with all her heart: "My God, if life is meant to have beauty and meaning, then how can I live without seeing his beautiful, loving eyes again; a love that flows through his hand to mine, from his soul to mine? Don't let me lose him, my God; please bring him back to me."

Within moments, a blinding flash of light revealed a brilliant white angelic figure, with glorious, translucent wings, soaring up into the open sky from deep within the castle. The little human butterfly, deep in prayer, suddenly realized that her very own mother was flying above her, holding the badly wounded and bleeding Tristan in her arms.

The human butterfly was completely incredulous. "Can this really be you, mother? Why have you never come to me before? Why have you never told me the truth of how I was born? Is it true that you were born in a town called Magdala near the Sea of Galilee? Is your real name Mary?"

"None of that matters now. I died during childbirth and was immediately resurrected as an angel before you were actually born. The Angel of Death flew into my room and raped me in the middle of the night while I was sleeping. He was drawn to me because of the demons that once wracked my soul. You were meant to be quickly aborted, but that's something I could never allow.

"You were born with green eyes and tiny wings. I've always loved you for your gentleness and your compassion. None of the other angels knows about you. None of them would know what to do with you. Neither do I. This must be our last conversation. I'm leaving you with a gift that honors the beauty of your soul. As I leave you now, I want you to look up at the sky."

"But, leave my Tristan with me, mother. I'm not an angel. Now that I've fallen in love with him I can't live without him."

"He's very near death. That's how I was able to rescue him from the castle. If he dies before the end of our journey he'll have to be resurrected immediately. I won't be able to help you. Only you can bring him back with your kiss. You can't do it in this evil place. I'll protect you from the Count, but it's up to you now to protect your brave warrior. In the meantime, look up at the sky."

At that moment, the heavens opened to a massive canvas of circling butterflies immersed in swirling rainbows of color, flowing through unimpeded moonlight far above the castle. Red, blue, green, yellow, white, magenta, purple butterflies by the thousands, along with massive brown monarchs by the hundreds of thousands; swirling in spontaneous, uneven motion throughout every corner of their universe.

Her angelic mother had already begun her journey, flying at blinding speed with Tristan in her arms; but the little butterfly could sense that her mother was communicating to her telepathically.

"You've found someone who's worthy of you, my beautiful daughter. A warrior unlike any other. He's fallen deeply in love with you. I'm grateful that the two of you have already tasted the love potion together. I'm carrying your lover to a green field far away. I want you to meet him there. I've chosen Ireland because it's the place most blessed in this world, the place closest to heaven.

"Follow the butterflies, my darling; they'll guide you to your warrior. With your kiss, your love will last for all eternity. Your unusual need for sustenance will be addressed and provided for you. You must never ask where it comes from. All you need to know is that it's provided with great love from the fairies and leprechauns who live and thrive in this part of the world.

"Go now and fly to your beloved, my little butterfly. May the God of the angels be with you."

THE END

Bonnie's Dream

"All right, I get it. Somebody broke your heart. Endless loneliness. The days go by in droves. A lifetime ends up as nothing more than a stutter, or sometimes just a blink. I get it. A lot of us do. Memories get blurred when you peer back through the frayed edges of your meaningless life, like a mosquito gliding through a filter of forgotten dreams.

"A broken heart? Of course. More than once? Probably. What would a meaningful life look like without an occasional broken heart? You have friends; kind of; maybe. You're attractive, but that doesn't really get you much. An oppressive loneliness resides at the bottom of every soul.

"So, the question is: why are you screwing your life up like this? Why do you keep getting into trouble with the law? Why can't you map out a normal life like everybody else? Is emptiness really that unbearable? The emptiness of all those days in droves?

"Let's dispense with the platitudes for a minute. How about you spill something right out of your gut? What can you tell me about life? C'mon, Bonnie, quote me some of your special poetry. I hear you're pretty good at it. What gives life meaning for you? Or better yet, why is there such a lack of meaning in your life? The answer to that last question should tell me all I need to know.

"Actually, forget it. I already know why you're so damned depressed. You're just like all the rest of us. You've been craving the right person to share your life with. And it's not that you haven't tried. They tell me you got married to your high school sweetheart before you even turned 16.

"Hell, if I heard right, you're still married to the loser. He's up at the penitentiary at Huntsville.

"I don't think you really know what the hell you want, Bonnie, but it's time for you to get your shit together. What are you now, 18? 19? I'm going to let you in on a little secret. Most of us who reside in this dirty little town learned this a long time ago. It's our depressing, small town truth.

"Are you ready for some hard truth? The right person may not even exist. Not for you. Not ever.

"Damn, you're not looking too good, Bonnie. You really tied one on, didn't you. Are you gonna throw up? Let me get someone to walk you over to the toilet in case you need to puke your guts out. Why do I get the feeling you're a little disgusted with me right now, or is it just the law you're fed up with.

"I'll tell you what … get in there and take care of whatever it is you need to do, and then I'll let you go home and sleep it off. I'll get you a ride home. Just sign this for me so I can show that I'm doing my job. But stay away from the booze, for Christ's sake. I don't know where you're getting it, and I don't care. The next time they drag you in here for being drunk on your ass in public, I'll let you sleep it off in a jail cell."

Signed,
Bonnie Parker
January 6th, 1930
Sheriff's Dept.
West Dallas, TX

It seems that Bonnie had developed a rather overwhelming taste for alcohol. An honor student who loved to write poetry, now she's working as a waitress; but when she gets off work she'll head right for the booze. Prohibition is still the law of the land, but alcohol isn't really that hard to find. It's just a matter of who you know.

When the booze gets into her veins, she starts to feel that life might be worth living after all. After the police dropped her off she found herself slipping away to another world. Tomorrow was going to be hangover time. Splitting headache. The works.

Her dream placed her smack in the middle of a bank robbery; loud and chaotic with a woman screaming, shots being fired, a bank guard lying on the floor in a pool of blood. Bonnie had never fired a gun, but now she was holding one. A colt .38 snub nose that fit in her hand like a glove.

"The cop's bleeding out, Floyd! Let's get the hell out of here!"

The robbers stumbled to the door with multiple sacks of cash, heading for their Ford Model A, driving off with guns blazing.

Pretty Boy Floyd! thought Bonnie. Wow! But the other guy was even prettier. Baby Face Nelson? No, not that pretty. Buck, I heard someone called. But it wasn't Buck. I can't remember.

She realized that she had been attracted to the sexy young bank robber in her dream. She wondered if maybe he had the same kind of feelings for her. She thought he actually smiled at her while he was holding up the bank manager. More like a goofy grin.

As with all her dreams, there wasn't much left to remember when she woke up in the morning with her splitting, booze inflicted headache. A hot cup of coffee might help; maybe not. The funny thing though: it was always the same dream. Running for their lives after robbing a bank.

Yeah, I'm fed up with the law all right. So, I was an "honor" student in high school. Everybody loved my poetry. Big deal. Now I'm a waitress. What good is it getting me? The guys in my dreams are the ones creating a little excitement. Where's the "honor" in being an honor student?

Bonnie knew that she was never going to marry a bank teller. She was going to rob a bank teller; scare a bank teller; humiliate a bank teller if need be, but get the money. She wouldn't have to be a waitress any longer. Just find the right guy to share the excitement with. The guy in her dreams.

Within a few hours she learned that she had lost her job as a waitress. They found out about her embarrassing exploits on the street the night before, when she loudly tried to pick up a guy delivering flowers to another young beauty. She wanted the flowers and she wanted the guy's attention. After all, in her mind she was every bit as attractive as the other woman. Finally, after a lot of commotion, the cops pulled up and arrested her for public drunkenness.

She broke down and cried profusely when she was arrested. Her despair and brutal loneliness had overwhelmed her, physically and emotionally. She knew that she would never see her husband again, but she would wear his wedding ring for the rest of her life.

A day or two later, after recovering from her hangover, she began to search for another job as a waitress. She was broke, and work was sparse for a young woman living in Texas in 1930.

Fortunately, she ran into a sympathetic friend who told her she could stay with her at her home while she was looking for work. This gave Bonnie a chance to feel normal for a little while, to hopefully find a little peace of mind. She even had her own bed.

Bonnie was a pretty little thing. Four foot ten, maybe 85 pounds. Smart and a very creative poet with talent as well for public speaking. What she really wanted was to be an actress. Talkies had been out for a while now and, oh lord, was it exciting. To be a movie actress, to be famous; but how would she get there? Didn't know anyone. No money; no job. Just keep her head down and try to find a job. But, oh, was she lonely.

"Someone's at the door, Bonnie. Can you grab it?"

"Sure, I'll get it … just a minute … It's a guy; kind of handsome. Do you know him?"

"Let me look … Yeah, I know him. He's a friend of my brother."

"Damn, he's actually … kind of hot. Does your brother have any other friends?"

"One at a time, Bonnie. I'm not real happy with this guy. He's always in trouble with the law. Go ahead, open the door for him."

"Well, hello little tiny person. I bet you're a friend of Christine's … Is Charlie home? … Hey, I'd just like to know something … Where did you get those big, beautiful blue eyes?"

"They just kind of show up. Every time I'm sober."

"Whoa! How often is that?"

"Every once in a while."

"Aren't you going to invite me in?"

"I'm thinking about it."

"Don't mind her, Clyde. She likes to joke around. I'll be out in a minute."

Christine's hot friend sauntered in and flopped lazily on the couch.

"So, what are you doing here?"

"Christine was kind enough to let me stay here while I'm looking for a job."

"So, what do you do?"

"I'm an actress."

"What?"

"I'm a waitress. I bet you didn't even know that talkies were out."

"Where are you a waitress at?"

"I guess I'm not anymore. I'm looking."

"Hey, why don't you let me take you out for breakfast? I've got a little money."

"Well … I don't …"

"It's all right, honey. Go out with him and get something to eat. Charlie's still in bed, anyway. He was out all night. Were you with him, Clyde?"

"Who, me? Not a chance. I always go to bed real early so I can get up early to go to church."

"Yeah, right. Go ahead, you two. Enjoy yourselves."

"C'mon, cutie. Let's get some grub."

The breakfast date didn't actually work out too well. Clyde reached over and put his hand way up under her skirt so he could attempt to stroke her private parts while they were having breakfast. She gave him an absolutely ferocious slap across the face. Made him smile.

"Damn, you pack some power in that little tiny arm."

"I don't need you to tell me that. Just keep your hands to yourself. You weren't invited."

"I suppose you're right there. Damn, my face still burns."

And so began the beginning of Bonnie and Clyde. Another hard slap or two over the next couple of days, and then a really hard, all-embracing physical encounter a few days later, which of course led to several more hard, all-embracing physical encounters. Way too much booze.

Bonnie loved to drink and Clyde loved to steal. How else would they find the money for her booze?

Bonnie soon learned that Clyde was very proficient with guns. That's all he talked about in the early days of their relationship. He had recently been sitting in jail, along with his brother Buck, for stealing a truckload of turkeys; but now, a few weeks later, he was back behind bars. A little more serious this time.

Bonnie was hooked on him by now. Really hooked. He begged her to sneak a gun into his jail cell. It appeared that he was about to be sent up to Huntsville for a long sentence, and he really needed to escape before they moved him. She finally said she'd try to do it for him, but she made him promise that he'd do everything in his power to stay out of trouble after this so they could have a life together. He said of course he would, he would absolutely do just that.

Somehow the gun escapade worked. Clyde escaped, but he was recaptured quickly. This time he was immediately sent to Eastham State Farm near Huntsville, a notoriously brutal prison where the guards would just as well kill you as look at you. You meant nothing to them. In fact, you meant nothing to anyone.

Clyde was sentenced to four years of hard labor. Within a short time he was overpowered and brutally raped several times by a psychopathic, bullish prisoner. Clyde eventually found a way to murder his torturer with a lead pipe. Another convict offered to take the rap as he was already in for life with no chance of parole.

Bonnie's alcoholism seemed out of control while Clyde was out of commission. She managed to find some work as a waitress, but was otherwise fairly incapacitated, living through her dreams. One night she alighted from her dreamworld and found herself in the presence of what must have been a spaceship out in the fields of rural Texas.

An imposing man with intense, "creepy" eyes walked down the ramp and out into the vast, empty fields. He was followed by a couple of young men who were attempting to help their elderly mother down the ladder. The man with the creepy eyes walked right up to her.

"We've been looking for you. The boys' mother thinks you're quite attractive. They take good care of her, but she thinks you'd make a nice addition to the family. That's Ma Barker and her boys. I'm Alvin Karpis. The people out there like to call me Creepy Karpis. They think my eyes look right through them.

"Mr. Hoover officially made me Public Enemy #1. Can you imagine that? He told a lot of people that he's going to capture me himself. He's such a weasely little creep. He'll piss his pants before he even gets close to me. I've killed a lot of men. That's a little scary to a man like J. Edgar."

"Mr. Karpis, my boyfriend's still at Eastham State Farm. I told him I'll wait for him. I don't even want to live anymore if I don't have someone to love; someone to love me."

"I think I know him. You two are really going to make a splash. You're going to be even bigger than our gang, the Ma Barker/Alvin Karpis gang. Just remember to stay true to yourself, little lady. That's all any of us really has: that determination to never let anyone else try to run your life. Just remember, you're a personal friend of Alvin Karpis. I'll always be here for you."

"Don't you need to get back to the ship?"

"We're already on the ship," replied Ma Barker. "I don't expect you to understand, honey. By the way, that guy you're attached to is a savage. I've heard that he likes to make fun of people who go to church. Me and my boys go to church every Sunday. The only time we'll miss it is when we're running from the law. I always carry my bible with me. Do you want to see it?"

Bonnie could make out only four words as she stared at the open book: "Thou shalt not kill."

Alvin Karpis and the Barkers all faded from her dream, but the ship remained. Bonnie was so tired and hungover that she could barely stand, yet in her dream she found herself slowly climbing the ladder up onto the ship. After stumbling through a few empty rooms she suddenly found herself right smack in the middle of a marathon dance contest. It looked like it might have been going on for several days. Everyone was beyond exhausted. Several couples had collapsed on the floor as the music continued to play. Others were asleep in each other's arms, but still barely standing.

Bonnie found herself in the arms of an extremely handsome stranger who seemed eager to hold on to her. He was so imposing that she found herself staring straight up into his dark blue eyes. His eyes were almost as intense as those of Alvin Karpis, but nothing creepy this time; just overwhelmingly sexy. He introduced himself as John Dillinger. She recognized the name. An infamous bank robber and killer. Pretty Boy Floyd and Baby Face Nelson were part of his gang.

She and the great John Dillinger held on tight to each other as both tried to keep their balance, but it was hopeless. They ended up collapsing into each other's arms; and, after a lingering, passionate kiss, fell fast asleep on the dance floor. During a troublesome sleep, which seemed to last for several hours, she woke up to the sound of a man snoring. She bumped him slightly with her elbow, teasing him to stop, but then she realized it was she who was doing the snoring. The famous John Dillinger had abandoned her. He was nowhere in sight..

Her morning headache, as usual, was pretty intense. Two cups of coffee helped ease the pain, but the idea of having to go out and look for work was debilitating in itself. Within a few hours she found herself drowning in her usual stupor while lying on the couch in her mother's home in West Dallas.

A loud knocking slowly began to burst through her consciousness. Somebody or something was standing outside on the porch. The knocking was intense and persistent. She had no choice but to try to answer the door.

Her mother got to the door first. "Clyde broke out of prison, but he can't stay here in Texas. He's on the run. Tell Bonnie that he'll send for her. Tell her to relax; he'll get a message to her." Then the two friends took off in their Ford Model A without looking back.

By now, Clyde realized that no amount of friends, no amount of freedom, could ever make up for not having Bonnie by his side. He was hooked on Bonnie from the bottom of his soul. What other reason could there be to go on living? In prison he had learned to hate, but through Bonnie he was learning to love from the very depths of his humanity. Bonnie felt exactly the same way. In her mind, they were now connected to the end of time.

Bonnie got the word through Clyde's two local friends that he was hiding out in a small town in Oklahoma, just north of the Texas border. He wanted her to hitchhike up to the border so he could arrange to meet her where it would be much harder for the Texas authorities to get to him. Bonnie's mother tried to talk her out of it, but it was hopeless. Bonnie and Clyde were now one.

She began to plan her trip, but what was there to plan? She couldn't really carry anything. Clyde sent word for her not to worry about clothing. His intentions were simply to steal whatever she needed, whatever she wanted. The beginning of the Great Depression was starting to be recognized for what it was to become: Hell on earth, especially for the farmers and sharecroppers throughout the dust bowl. Banks would continue to close and suicides would continue to rise.

Bonnie and Clyde soon found their way back to each other's arms and quickly began their two year flight through bank robberies, filling station robberies, and multiple grocery store stick-ups. The amount of money collected didn't matter so much to Clyde; it was just that he needed to get enough money for them to live.

They had developed a habit of visiting friends and family while on the run. They'd just show up in regular neighborhoods to visit them. If they ran into trouble, so be it. That's what guns are for.

Murder started to come easy for Clyde, who always kept his loaded Colt .45 in his waistband. Over time, Bonnie started to keep a gun with her as well, a .38 snub-nose detective special that she kept taped to the inside of her thigh with white medical tape.

Sometimes someone had to die, and the two of them would have to run for their lives. Life's an adventure after all. We'll just have to keep it moving. Find another cash register and maybe we can get a bite to eat.

Clyde's older brother, Buck, along with his wife, Blanche, joined up with Bonnie and Clyde to form what became known as the Barrow gang. Buck was severely wounded later by sheriff's deputies, tipped to their whereabouts, who were trying to trap them in an apartment building.

Clyde came out firing and killed two deputies, but Buck was shot in the head as they were all running for their car. He lay dying for several days. Blanche refused to leave her husband though she was severely injured as well, taking glass in her eyes from a shattered windshield.

Bonnie and Clyde were on the run, leaving a trail of pain and despair throughout the heartland. Clyde became enamoured with the new Ford V8 which represented a huge improvement on the automobile landscape. Faster, easier to maneuver, and much more efficient for their escapes. He even wrote a letter intended for Henry Ford with glowing compliments for the new machine.

Clyde Barrow was a satisfied client of this magnificent achievement. He especially liked the ease of stealing one and driving it off in a blaze of thunder.

From time to time, a panoply of punks and semi-degenerates would line up to join the fun, as the Barrow gang would occasionally have to expand their outfit with perhaps two or three gentlemen of dubious repute, to be employed specifically for bank robberies. Over time, trust would become an issue, as in "How well do you know these guys?" Meanwhile, Bonnie continued to live out her passion for alcohol. She kept the gun taped to her thigh, but she never fired it and prayed she'd never have to.

Yet she loved the excitement of being a gun moll. Bonnie and Clyde always kept a camera with them, and Bonnie loved to pose for pictures. These were meant for their private enjoyment only, but several of the more spicy ones were uncovered and eventually found their way to major newspapers.

Two in particular were spread throughout the country. One had Bonnie posing as a hardened gun moll in a sexy pose, with gun in hand, while smoking a cigar. The other had her holding a rifle up against Clyde's chest. Clyde seemed to be enjoying this as a slight smile was beginning to break across his face. The irony for them, of course, was that Bonnie had never smoked a cigar and had no intention of ever smoking one.

Things would get harder and harder for them over the next several months, as they were fiercely hunted by law enforcement officers throughout several states. A severe car accident while Clyde was barreling down the highway, after eluding the police, caused a great deal of pain for Bonnie during the last year of her life.

Bonnie was trapped in the front seat of their car as battery acid poured out onto her leg, burning her flesh all the way down to the bone. From then on she could hardly walk, and Clyde had to carry her most of the time. Prohibition had ended by then, and Clyde was able to steal enough alcohol for Bonnie to attempt to numb the pain so she could get through each day. But now, she had to spend most of her time in the seat of the latest Ford V8 that Clyde had been able to steal.

One very dark night in the fields outside of Baton Rouge, Bonnie fell into a drunken stupor. She wasn't even able to leave the car and step out into the fields to relieve herself. She was virtually incapacitated. In her dream, she was greeted by the darkest angel in the firmament; an angel with pure black wings as well as a black tongue and black lips.

Bonnie asked if she had died and gone to Hell. The angel answered that Bonnie had been living in Hell throughout her life, so what difference did it make? Bonnie answered that she had escaped from Hell a couple of times during her lifetime: The first time, when her abusive husband abandoned her when she was just sixteen; and, more recently, the moment when she realized that Clyde would be the one who was promised to her by God.

The dark angel asked her if she really thought she knew who God was. Bonnie answered that she only knew that God is forever; that all her prayers would have been empty if she didn't know who she was praying to. "I never went to Sunday School. I just went out into the fields and learned that I was never alone."

At that moment, Clyde, who had been tricked by a former associate to stop and help him with car trouble, began to run back to Bonnie, who was sitting in the front seat of their Ford V8. He was cut down almost immediately by intense, overwhelming gunfire from the brush where they had stopped to help. Bonnie realized for a brief moment, as she glanced into the eyes of her beloved, that she was about to die. They found later that 130 rounds had been fired into their car.

God's will won out that day; and it was all right. Sometimes we don't get to make the rules. It was as God intended for Bonnie and Clyde.

THE END

The Spanish Steps

A lone figure walking through the shadows of Rome, grieving bitterly, suddenly finds himself at the bottom of the Spanish Steps. There's nowhere else to go. She's gone, and so am I.

I wasn't sure if we'd be able to climb the steps. Remember, honey, how we talked about it? But if you were here with me we certainly would have tried. What kind of a life would we have if we decided to give up before attempting to climb the steps? To reach the top of somewhere. Anywhere. But you have now, my darling. You've reached Heaven, haven't you.

So many people have experienced the Spanish Steps. How many others have died here? Untold thousands, I would imagine. Respighi and his Pines of Rome. Puccini and his Tosca. The intoxicating beauty of the music of Rome filtering through the centuries. The history of Rome forever bursting through our memories. But now it's over. Rome is nothing more than a bleak reminder of our broken past.

As I stand here at the base of the steps, I can feel your arms around me. I sense that two people in love hold more power in their hands than all the untold poor souls who have climbed these steps before them. But one isn't enough. It takes two. The need to love and the need to be loved.

How will I find you now, my love? I'll never stop loving you, but how will I know that you still love me? Are you in a place where you're still able to love me? I need your love so desperately.

The broken figure broke down and began to weep, falling to his knees on the unkempt streets of Rome. People passed him by. Mobs of tourists passed by. Where were they coming from? Didn't they know that people die on these steps everyday?

He began to crawl upward on his hands and knees, painfully attempting to navigate one step at a time. This simple act is prohibited by a city ordinance that forbids lounging, even sitting, on the Spanish Steps. Walking up or down the steps at a regular pace is acceptable, but lingering is never allowed.

After a few minutes the police arrived. Four men in uniform surrounded him to ask him if he was all right. They were somewhat baffled as to why he kept trying to climb the steps, even while they were talking to him. His knees had to be very sore by now. His legs were gnarled and painful looking.

"Please stop moving, Signore, while we're talking to you. Where do you think you're going?"

"Directly to Heaven. I intend to break every rule on earth."

"If you refuse to abide by our laws we may have to arrest you."

"I might not let that happen."

"It appears that your legs have been injured in an accident. Is that why you're trying to crawl up the steps?"

"It happened right here at the base of the steps. My wife and I were celebrating our anniversary. We were just out for a stroll."

"Of course, I remember now. It happened just days ago. Please accept our condolences. Is there anything we can do to assist you?"

"You can leave me alone. I'm going to crawl up to the top of the steps to be with my wife. Just leave me a clear path on the right side, close enough to the Keats-Shelley house so that John Keats can see me from his window. He'll understand why I'm attempting to climb the steps. I suspect that he knows my wife very well by now. They've had many beautiful conversations over the past several days. He died from tuberculosis in 1821 at only 25 years of age. His whole life should have been in front of him.

"Yes, Signore, we've all heard the stories. We live here, after all."

"The beautiful inscription on his gravestone reads that his name was 'writ in water."

"Signore, let us help you to a facility to get some treatment. You're not well."

"I'm stronger than all the rest of you put together. All I need from you is a little understanding. I'm going to crawl all the way to the top to be with my wife."

"You know we can't let you attempt to do that."

"How do you intend to stop me?"

"We've already called for a van to take you to the hospital."

"Then you're in for a big disappointment. Do you really want to cause a scene?"

"All right, they're just pulling up. Just be sensible and come with us peacefully. You need help."

"Keats and Shelley are coming with me. We've all lived desperately poetic lives. Do you understand what that means?

"I understand that you're a nutcase, my poor friend. Nobody here has time for this. They're ordering me to leave a couple of officers here to keep an eye on you. They don't want us carting you off in front of people."

"I've got a much better idea. Go dig up a news crew to film my journey. As bad as my legs are, it's going to take me more time than it should; but this is front page stuff, gentlemen. This could get you some wonderful notoriety. Get the news crew out here. Let me talk to them."

"They're not going to talk to you. I don't know if you've noticed, but all these people out here on the street are laughing at you."

"That shows I can draw a crowd. Get me the TV crew. Hell, they're already here. Look!"

"Gentlemen! What's going on here? We heard there's a lot of commotion out here on the steps. So, what's going on?"

"This poor American is a nutcase. He just lost his wife. We all feel sorry for him. We've been trying to get him into the van so we can get him some help."

"So, what's the problem, Signore? Why are you causing all this commotion?"

"I'm going to crawl to the top of the steps. I believe my wife is waiting for me up there. My legs are bad, so it won't be easy, but I can do it with your help."

"How can we possibly be of help to you?"

"You can help me by getting permission for me to climb these steps, at my own pace, without being hassled. All I ask is that you do it quickly. I intend to start my journey in a matter of minutes. You can follow me with your cameras and put it on the air tomorrow night. Your ratings will go through the roof. I want the world to experience the power of God's love."

"How does God figure into it?"

"God figures into every breath we take. Of course, when we stop breathing God becomes irrelevant. Is that what you believe?"

"That's not exactly what I meant; it's just that I'm not religious. I guess you can call me a classic newshound. Give me a few minutes to make the call. Let's see what I can do."

"Get me permission to linger briefly in Keats's quarters before I start. Is there a cafeteria in his building?"

"There's anything and everything, Signore. In Rome there are dreams around every corner."

"Then so shall it be."

"I'm sorry about the loss of your wife. From what I understand, a group of drunk university students came roaring down the streets, flying around the corner, and there you were. You seemed to have managed pretty well, but your wife … I'm so sorry. The families should be responsible for making restitution to you for your terrible loss."

"I have to say, your English is pretty good, much better than my Italian. Plus, you seem to be smarter than you look. It'll be a big help to me if you'll personally accompany me up the steps, at least from a short distance."

"I don't know if that's possible; I have other assignments. I lead a full news team."

"But you can make it happen."

"You're quite stubborn and demanding, Signore. You should realize that people don't always …"

"Do you believe in angels on earth?"

"What? Why would you ask such a ridiculous question? You're way off the deep end here. Are you trying to suggest that we're surrounded by …?

"You're looking at one."

"Looking at what?"

"Just stand there for a minute and clear your mind. Do you believe in angels on earth?

"I'm not sure if I understand what that means."

"If I have to explain it to you, then I guess I've picked the wrong man."

"Explain what, exactly?"

"Something I've always known, but I've never told a soul; not even my wife."

"This is crazy … The officer was right. You need to be in a hospital."

"Are your feet starting to burn? You can feel the smoke, but you won't see it; and once it starts, you can't put it back quite the way it was. I've been advised by doctors that they can only repair my legs through surgery, but I'm telling you I could fly up these steps within seconds."

"This is getting ridiculous. I don't believe you."

"I'm about to lift you a quarter inch off the ground. Your feet will never again touch the ground while you're standing still. The people around you won't notice, but you will."

"That's absolutely crazy. Where are your wings?"

"The ability to fly comes from within. Now go take care of my request. We're about to start climbing. The smoke won't last, but you'll never again touch the ground while you're standing still. Do you want to test me some more?"

"All right, give me a few minutes. I'll see if I can get permission. They'll refuse at first, but I'll tell them you're the one who was in that terrible accident the other night that killed your wife and damaged your legs. I think they'll want to get behind you … especially when I tell them that my crew will be filming you for television."

"Then what are we waiting for? Direct me to Keats's room. I want to look out his window. I want to see exactly what he saw. I want to envision what he saw with that beautiful mind of his. I want to imagine that he may have noticed me when he looked out his window. I may have been the muse for some of his writings."

"Keep those thoughts to yourself, Signore. They'll come back to lock you up in the nuthouse."

"Then I'll have to show them who I really am. I don't think I want to do that."

"I don't think that would be advisable."

"Hmm … you're actually starting to come around; and your English really is pretty good. The right words at the right time. I think I might have to keep you around for a while. Now let's make this official. Be sure to let the police know about this. No hassles while I'm climbing!

"I'll be right back, Signore. My crew will stay with me until it starts to get dark. Can you make it up to the top by then?"

"Perhaps not. My legs are really sore. I may have to lean back and rest on one of the steps after you leave later tonight. We can pick it up in the morning. Make sure the police all know about it. Street cleaners too."

"We'll get started as soon as we can. I think you can do it."

"I know I can do it, but how long will it take is the question."

"Actually, I think we're almost ready. The question is … are you ready?

"Give me a quick restroom break and a quick snack. I'll take a look at Keats's room on the way up. The rest is up to God."

After crawling upward for a few minutes, he arrived at Keats's apartment. The poetry was startling. The air was on fire with Keats's legacy. Percy Bysshe Shelley was there too. He was not only an immaculately beautiful poet, but his wife, Mary Shelley, was a brilliant novelist.

The next few hours were exceedingly painful. Crawling laboriously while dragging his gnarled and distorted legs, he continued to inch and scrape his way along the hard, rigid concrete leading up to the sky. At last, about three quarters of the way up the Spanish Steps, he allowed himself to turn and briefly observe the crowd following him.

He was shocked to see his wife's killers among the crowd. All three of them. He knew who they were. They were driven simply by an insane curiosity to see the damage they had created. For the first time in his life he decided to expose his true identity and take matters into his own hands. There was no reason to hide it from the world any longer.

As his earthly body completely collapsed near the top step, he could feel his skin beginning to unravel into smoldering pieces of soft, evaporating scales, foaming into a pure, feathery white cream, then slowly evolving into huge and gloriously majestic wings; wings so powerful that you couldn't carve through them with even the most brutal of blades. Within moments he stood on his previously gnarled feet and extended his newfound wings, which were now expanding into magnificent seventeen foot long wings of the Gods.

"God will forgive them, but I never will."

With that chilling declaration, the lone figure folded his wings in front of him before thrusting them out onto the Spanish Steps. The three college students began to panic. Each was targeted and lifted high up into the air, tumbling heavily over each other, floating into a confusing mix of wonderment and amazement, before falling onto the pavement into a cacophony of blood-curdling screams.

The lone figure had suddenly transformed into a God; or was it a Devil; a terrifying behemoth of biblical proportions. No one could stand near him; no one could enter his presence. He was all things and nothing at all: The Leviathan as prophesied in the Bible.

He began to randomly pull out large clumps of hair from each of the three screaming young men before realizing that he was out of his element. He was not of the Devil. He could hear the voice of John Keats whispering to him that it was never about him. It was about God.

In spite of all the pain he had caused, he was finally able to come to his senses and realize that he was never meant to be an angel. He knew at that moment that he never intended to hurt anyone. He never actually saw the three students or transformed into an evil presence; he just imagined it.

Now realizing he was entirely filled with God's love, he noticed his wife standing near the top of the steps, eagerly awaiting his arrival. He felt for his legs. They were strong and steady. He could walk freely. Of course he could. Why wouldn't he be able to walk freely?

He was suddenly overcome with the angelic beauty of his wife, who was waiting patiently for him to reach the top of the steps. He realized that his wife was the true angel. She had always been the true angel. God, grant me the wisdom to accept what I must have known all along. Our accident the other night was not really an accident. It was God's will. It was our time.

He finally reached the peak of the Spanish Steps. His wife's beauty was overwhelming. She had been touched by God. He stood entranced as he watched her from a slight distance. After a minute he went to her, walking easily and freely. They embraced passionately, holding hands with infinite tenderness under the umbrella of God's love. For a few moments they stared deeply into each other's eyes, then slowly turned and walked into the clouds of Heaven together.

The news crew picked up all their equipment and started loading the van to leave the area.

"Wait a minute. Where are my feet? I can't feel the ground."

"What do you mean, you can't feel the ground?"

"I'm standing here, but I don't feel anything!"

"You look fine to me."

"That's the point. I look fine, but I'm not."

"Sorry to see that your night crawler collapsed and died before he made it to the top. But where did they take his body? I didn't see him at the top of the steps. It's like he just disappeared. We need to find him. This could be a much bigger story than we thought. We can't even put it on the air. There's no proof that he even made it to the top."

"There's proof, but we can't use it."

"So where in the hell did he go?"

"I don't think he went to hell, but we might have."

"Maybe he ended up in Heaven. Was he some kind of a saint?"

"How would I know? I think I dozed off while he was resting. I must have dreamed this, but I could swear that he grew some kind of gigantic wings in place of his arms. It was about the same time when those three young men started screaming and carrying on. What was that all about?"

"Some things are better left unsaid. I know we're all getting paid for this, but I think we should just pack it up and forget this ever happened. We've got the tape of the whole thing, but what are we going to do with it? We can't tell our audience that he just disappeared."

"In the meantime, damn it, I can't feel the pavement beneath my feet."

"You know, it's almost six in the morning. The sun's coming up. Let's just get out of here. After all, it's just another glorious day on the Spanish Steps."

"Here, let's all have a sip. Let's drink to the man who crawled all the way up the Spanish Steps and then simply disappeared."

"I think I just got a glimpse of John Keats. He just winked at me."

"All right, let's get out of here."

THE END

Angels of Ushuaia

The end of the world. Everybody knows where it is; a few piles of rocks in southern Argentina; scant hours of daylight in the winter; a multitude of black, somber skies.

Welcome to Ushuaia. The southernmost city in the world. A nice town, actually. But how many boats have crashed on the rocks of Cape Horn?

You say you're just going for a ride? West/East? East/West? Drake Passage? The Straits of Magellan? Or maybe all the way around South America; around Cape Horn.

Might be a little rough. You might have to barf a little; probably more than a little. But so what? The scenery is dynamic. Glaciers. The works. Keep going southward and you'll find yourself stuck in the middle of the most brutal weather on earth: Antarctica.

It all started because you wanted to get involved with a little card game.

"Do you really have to go out again tonight, Bill? Can't you spend just a little time with me? It gets so lonely here by myself. You're always in such a hurry."

"Ahh, it's just a little card game. It's too easy to get hooked on poker. I keep saying enough, enough, enough; but you get a little rush going and you don't want to get up and leave."

"There are people in this town who want to see you dead, Bill. They mean it. People are talking. I've heard that tempers really start to boil over when you're in there. Can't you just take a little breather tonight and come sit with me for a while?"

"They all know me. They know my reputation. They know I can outgun any of them. Outshoot any of them. I guess that's supposed to give them an excuse to just mosey on down to the saloon and plug me in the back. You know I always insist on facing the door when I'm playing."

"That's not good enough, my love. Why take so many chances?"

"I can't change who I am, sweetheart. I've never shown an ounce of fear to anyone in my life. Why start now? They can all kiss my sweaty, slimy .32 caliber Smith and Wesson if they don't like it. That's what I'm carrying tonight."

A little after 8:00 pm, a couple who were out walking on the sidewalk reported a scream coming from a house down the street. The woman who lived there had been brutally attacked, raped and left for dead. Her husband had been playing poker. After learning that his wife had been brutalized, he ran out into the street and immediately went gunning for the monster who did this. He knew what the killer looked like through several passersby' descriptions, but the coward had immediately disappeared. People on the street had seen him riding full speed out of town, never to return.

They said his name was John Wesley Hardin, an infamous killer and gunfighter, but seemingly impossible to track down. He yelled out that they'd never find him. But one man would soon be coming for him; even to the ends of the earth.

The funeral took place the next day. Everybody knew everybody else. Ashes to ashes, dust to dust. The words were overly familiar to the farmers and drifters in this small, prairie town in South Dakota. So many people had been cut down within a moment's notice, or lack of notice.

But, how was this different? Such a brutal lack of remorse. A senseless lack of humanity. Who could possibly stand behind a decision like this? Does God turn his back when the devil decides to take his turn? Or does God simply not care about you or me? Is life meant to be so transient that literally nothing matters?

The kind reverend pronounced a few words of bereavement and the group quickly dispersed. Several of the wife's friends brought flowers to the grave. The husband stood calmly by himself. He had friends as well, but his neighbors hesitated to speak to him; nobody patted him on the shoulder. He was all alone.

He began to wonder if his tracking skills were still in order. There was no doubt that his gun skills were as strong as ever. He was known for being faster than lightning as well as possessing an uncanny accuracy that was almost beyond belief. It had been claimed recently by several witnesses that, after a quick draw, he had deposited six bullets into a six inch circle on a sign 50 to 60 yards away without using his pistol sights.

But now he was possessed with an evil beyond anything he had ever experienced before. It was completely out of character, but the evil appeared to have completely taken control of his life. He seemed to be driven by an evil Goddess who had captured his soul. She was driving him into an abyss; a wave of sentient spirits leading him through a cyclone of abject terror.

He knew he'd have to keep moving if he wanted to find even a shred of peace. He was drowning in his own fears. Fears that he had never had to face before. After all, he was known to be fearless.

John Wesley Hardin had a 24 hour head start. The most cunning of killers, with an extremely fast draw, who was brutally inclined to kill if necessary. But did it always have to be necessary?

Bill began to ride through the brush on the way out of town to see if he could pick up tracks from the vanished killer. As he continued riding, he wondered why they were so easy to pick up. Clear as a bell, larger than life, enhanced by the strong prairie breezes that swept through the area outside of town. It seemed to him that, with a multitude of rising storms, it should have been just the opposite.

After a few weeks of hard traveling and hard living he finally came to the end of the line: the South Pacific Ocean. He could see where John Wesley Hardin had changed horses several times on his journey to the sea, but Bill realized that the path had now been handed to him on a silver platter. He would simply board the seagoing vessel going to Ushuaia. He realized after his long journey that, for some reason, Ushuaia, at the end of the world, was to be his final destination.

Sometime during his first few days at sea, a young man walked up to him and introduced himself while they were out on deck.

"So, you're the man I've been waiting to see. So much larger than life. Maybe even larger than death. My name is Henry McCarty. Have you ever heard of me?"

"Hello son. I don't think I have. I'm just wondering what you're doing on this ship. It's so desolate out here. Where are you traveling to?"

"Any place will do. I'm not particular. I know why you're here, though. You're looking for John Wesley Hardin. I believe you just passed him in the corridor. You didn't see him, did you."

"Wait a minute … there's no way I could have missed him."

"He didn't want you to see him. That's why he didn't appear to you. I think he still has respect for you."

"Does that mean that you don't?"

"I'm going to have you for breakfast, old man. You're nothing but an over-the-hill, burnt out, old gunfighter. Speaking of names, you can call me Billy. Everybody else does."

"Am I supposed to know you, Billy?"

"All you need to know is that I'm about to take your life."

"Why would you want to do that, Billy? You're nothing more than a kid."

"How about you, old man? May I call you Billy as well?"

"Mr. Hickok will do just fine."

"All right, Mr. Hickok. You can call me Billy the Kid."

The two men each stepped backwards about ten feet while continuing to face each other, with their gun hands slightly out to the side. Billy drew first. He was fast, really fast, but he couldn't compete with Wild Bill Hickok. No one could … except perhaps John Wesley Hardin.

As he pulled out his gun, Billy the Kid turned out to be nothing more than an apparition. Bill Hickok had already drawn his gun and shot him through the chest. Nothing remained but a whiff of smoke.

"Mr. Hickok?"

"Who wants to know?"

"John Wesley Hardin. You've been following me for quite a while. Are you going to arrest me? Do you really think you can outdraw me?"

"You're going to have to pay for what you did to my wife."

"I never had the pleasure of meeting your wife."

"She was raped and murdered, you son-of-a-bitch!"

"Not by me. Sure, I was in Deadwood that night. I got into … shall we say a little discussion with a local rancher. He seemed to take offense at the idea of me sleeping with his wife. But I promise you, she didn't mind it a bit. He sent his whole crew after me; they came at me in a blitz. I had to ride out of town as fast as I could to keep from getting bushwacked. I kept moving because of all the damn wanted posters they've got out for me all over the country."

"Why should I listen to this? You're trying to tell me it wasn't you after all?"

"You should remember me, Marshal Hickok. We've met before. You once asked me to leave my guns at the Marshal's office in Abilene, which I did. They say I've killed over 20 men, but I always had a lot of respect for you. I'd never do anything like this."

"Then who was it?"

"Does it really matter anymore? You're on your way to hell; you must know that by now. You've been chasing a really dark dream. John Wesley Hardin is actually still alive. Billy the Kid is still alive. But you're not, Mr. Hickok. You've been chasing shadows. Your life was destroyed with a bullet to the back of your skull that night in the saloon.

"Think about it, Mr. Hickok. I heard the whole story. You didn't realize it at the time, but you humiliated an evil bastard by the name of Jack McCall earlier that day when you cleaned him out at Faro in the same saloon.

"Your mistake was in your kindness. You offered him money so he could get something to eat afterward. He accepted your offer, but that humiliated him even more. From what I heard, at that very moment he decided to kill you as soon as he could get you in a compromising position.

"I heard that when you came in that night to play there was only one chair available, and it was backing the door. You tried several times to get a player who was facing the door to trade places with you, but he adamantly refused."

"I don't believe any of this. I'd never sit with my back to the door."

"Let's see if this brings back any of your memory of that night."

John Wesley Hardin pulled out four cards and stuck them right in front of Marshal Hickok's face.

"I don't have the other card. I don't even know what it was. This is all I was given. I know this is painful, but does it jog your memory?"

Bill Hickok stared at two black aces and two black eights, then immediately whirled and fired his Smith and Wesson into the wall. He started to shake like a leaf as it all came rolling back to him. The ultimate nightmare. A bullet in the back of the head. A skull shattered like glass.

He began to stagger down the corridor, but his legs gave out and he collapsed on the floor. John Wesley Hardin had disappeared. Wild Bill Hickok was now all alone. As he leaned back against the bulkhead, a soft whisper began to flow through the back of his mind, expanding rapidly into the song of a thousand dead souls, all vibrating in perfect harmony. A choir of angels, perhaps? He was alone now with the memory of his recent death blistering throughout his mind.

So many people had admired and respected him during his lifetime, but now he was surrounded by only the Angels of Ushuaia. They seemed to be there to comfort him through his death journey. The ship was still moving. He could hear the waves calling him, trying to take him under. Would he end up at the bottom of the sea? Would the angels protect him?

He managed to get to his feet and slowly found his way along the bulkhead and out onto the deck. Through the haze he could see the Ushuaia encampment in the distance. It was now deep in the dark of night. The angels' song continued to flow through the waves. The soft, otherworldly lighting on shore was enhanced by the glow of the Ushuaia Angels.

He found himself staring into the breeze for what appeared to be an eternity. Perhaps it was. His concept of time was now lost forever. The continuous presence of angels was all that seemed to matter, flowing up through the waves into the last vestige of his earthly sanity.

Where would he go now? The ship was still moving. What could that mean? Was he really on his way to hell? Or had he already arrived?

A sudden storm began to release drops of liquid from far above the deck head, slowly dripping down to caress the top of his scalp until they found a narrow opening near the base of his skull. As he reached up with his gun hand, he could feel the emptiness that used to be the back half of his skull.

He began to realize that Ushuaia Angels were never angels at all. They were insidious demons. How could there be true angels this far south? Ushuaia was to be his last glimpse of civilization. For those who have committed egregious murders, the "angels" were there to "escort" you into the depths of hell.

They're going to be sorry they ever heard of me, he thought. I'm going to eliminate as many of them as possible. I'll confront all of them: their insane evil against my unyielding moral code. The code of the lawmen of the old west.

You think they'll laugh at me? They should be scared to death of a moral code that rewards right actions and deeply punishes evil. There's no debate about this. We never asked WHY you did it; only IF you did it. The moral code of the west of 1876 is what keeps civilization strong.

I know it looks to these so-called angels like I'm on my way to hell; but the truth is that only God can make that decision. I used a multitude of firearms to protect the gentle souls of Abilene. I outdrew and outshot a score of evil men over the years; but I regret none of it. I made a horrible mistake when my young deputy came up behind me to back me up during a gunfight in Abilene.

We all know that I turned and fired after taking out the evil bastard in front of me. But what else could I have done? It was all instinctive. I saw his shadow quickly running up behind me. He should have known to stay clear during a gunfight. We talked about situations like this when I hired him. He was my friend. That was the end of my career as a marshal; but even now, in my death, I stand behind the need for honest gunplay to maintain the peace and uphold the law.

Marshal Hickok knew that no one cared about any of this anymore. His life was over. He was on his way to hell. The ship had begun to slowly and ponderously turn toward portside, soon to be heading due south to drop off its one passenger; an ancient cargo ship with only one passenger.

So is this what hell looks like? he thought. No one to talk to? No one to interact with? Solitude beyond the boundaries of sanity? I guess I'll find out soon enough.

As the ship continued to turn, Jack McCall stepped out of the haze. He still had a noose hanging around his neck.

"Hello Mr. Hickok. I believe you're here to meet with the Angels of Ushuaia. I never liked you. You're too damn arrogant; too sure of yourself. You think you have the right to kill anyone you want. That's why I took off half of your skull. Can you feel the breeze blowing around in there?

"The Ushuaia Angels sent me here. We all have to follow their song. They don't have faces or bodies. They lead people into hell. We're all programmed to follow them when we die. Unless, of course, we all happen to be some kind of saints.

"They're the devil, Mr. Hickok. They're not real angels. I've never even seen a real angel. I'm sure I never will. The real angels are the ones who lead decent people up into heaven: preachers, bankers, store owners, school teachers, little old ladies who pray while doing their knitting."

"Tell me what happened to my wife."

"It wasn't me. After I put a bullet in your head I tried to hightail it out of town. Grabbed a horse but the damn saddle was loose and I hit the ground. Went running until they all came after me and grabbed me. Within a few days they gave me a phony trial and hanged me for killing you.

"They said it was John Wesley Hardin who raped your wife. He knew you were inside playing poker. I don't think he meant to kill her. He was putting the make on her."

"What are you doing on this ship?"

"I don't know. But the Ushuaia Angels didn't give me a choice. They never do. Just told me to get my ass over here. You can't kill me; I'm already dead. But they told me you're really going to work me over; you're really going to hurt me, Mr. Hickok. Actually, I think I might like that."

"Christ! I can't believe this. I must already be in hell. I'm on a ship with my killer."

"Your wife should be all the way up near the North Pole by now, waiting for you. I think your ship took a wrong turn. You ended up down here near the South Pole. I think they want us to head up there so you can try to see her. Your deputy's up there too. They told me I have to stick close to you."

"But, you're evil!"

"So are you."

Wild Bill hesitated for a long moment, as if pondering that last statement.

"Last call, Mr. Hickok. Are you going with me or not?"

"I … don't know …"

"Well, I do … can't you feel it? The ship's starting to move again. Damned if it doesn't feel like we're turning toward starboard. Grab a table … we can play Faro for as long as we want.

"Actually, I've been ordered by the Ushuaia Angels to play Faro with you … forever. But just remember, Mr. Hickok, you're not allowed to win; neither am I. You're always going to lose. That's what hell means."

THE END

The Visitors

At the peak of the highest mountain in the world, the largest angel in the firmament flows down to the peak at the stroke of midnight, then floats far above the edge. He's known to be the only angel who began his existence as a human, and yet he never experienced death. He was simply taken up to heaven by God.

He's beyond powerful, at God's right hand; and yet he realizes that he's powerless. He's simply God's messenger. He was chosen by God to clarify and perhaps instruct, but otherwise to never interact with humans. He was chosen by his creator to deliver God's message to all of us while we sleep. For God knows that his human creations have no ability to understand the glory and majesty of God's existence.

Humans are simply too weak to understand. We have no higher range of intelligence. In spite of what we may think, we were never created to be aware of God's presence. We can only understand God's message when we're asleep.

If we knew what we think we know, our minds would explode. God's loneliest angel is apparently our only hope of absorbing God's message.

He was never allowed to live in heaven with the rest of the angels. He was to live on the highest mountain peak on earth by fluttering above it. God instructed him to never allow himself to be seen, photographed, or recognized and, most importantly, to never touch down on earth. If he ever touched earth for even a moment, it might instigate a cataclysmic earthquake that could swallow up all of humanity. With that in mind, he was to remain vigilant night and day. He must never allow himself to sleep or rest.

Throughout the long history of civilization, God was never completely convinced of his decision to allow mere humanity the freedom to speak for him, in pulpits or otherwise; and yet, "free will" is the original basis of our existence, for God never wavers on his decisions. When a decision is made, it immediately becomes the law of nature.

"Free will" was one of his earliest decisions affecting humanity (I believe that Cain and Abel were still just toddlers), and it would seem that God is determined to stick with this decision all the way through the end of time. You and I have choices.

But the lonely angel was never allowed to speak to anyone; to be with anyone; to show himself to anyone. He was lonely beyond all boundaries of pain and endurance. Think of a world where you can see people in the distance, but you can't reach out to them. They might recognize you from afar. They've seen you in their dreams, but they can't relate to you. They don't understand you. They don't love you.

In his absolute misery, he decided to rebel against his creator. He would elicit a response from one of us while we slept; a response far beyond anything promised to him by God. He would choose a beautiful woman who touched his heart; a woman engulfed in loneliness; a woman who needed him even more than he needed her; a woman who could only be saved by her love for a true angel of God. In his depth of despair, he realized that he could only be saved by the love of a beautiful woman of the earth.

He had been watching her for what seemed like forever, absorbing her unforgiving beauty from beyond the edges of the firmament, far above the heavens. She was one of the many thousands of beautiful women he had longed for during his lifetime. After all, he was still a man.

But gossip abounds within God's city of angels: the culmination of thousands of fluttering tongues inserting themselves into tales of hopelessly abated glory. Was there ever a time when angels lived heroic lives? If so, how would any of them know? It was so long ago.

The Heavenly Father will ask his flock to step up once again to become entrenched in heroic deeds. For all hell is about to break loose. An angel of God intends to defy his creator and take a mere mortal for his bride. This would be unsustainable and unacceptable for the proper balance and preservation of the universe. Unless this angel can be discovered and destroyed before he touches the highest peak, the city of angels will be in grave danger of perishing from the earth.

God will gather all the angels of the firmament to remind them of the true reason for their existence. They'll be told to continue to interact with the human race, to comfort and enlighten within the scope of their abilities; but, from this moment on, they'll be under extreme pressure to merge their collective energy into the destruction of the only human to ever become an angel.

They all knew of him, of course, though they were instructed to never gaze upon him. They had never known the reason for his existence.

The eyesight of a flight of angels eventually becomes the fulcrum of their existence. A thousand eyes would soon be calling the lonely angel home. They'll be told to look upon him with the force of the billions of stars throughout all the galaxies of the universe. The stars will then become the eyes of the angels. This lone angel will never be able to avoid the gaze of millions of God's angels.

But gossip continues to spew from the lips of the heavenly host. Why was this one angel banned from touching the earth? Why had he been ordered to live apart from everybody else? Why were we told to never look at him? A small group of archangels wondered aloud if God had somehow realized, perhaps at the beginning of time, that this one dark angel might actually be the personification of evil.

In truth, the dark angel's propensity for evil was staggering to even the God of the archangels. He would need to be turned by a loving God into a lonely angel who must never be allowed to inflict his powers of evil on humanity. But now, to prevent this from happening, he'll need to be destroyed quickly, before he can take his bride from the masses of humanity.

The city of angels was suddenly alight with excitement, for boredom had become deeply entrenched over the millennia. "We needed this!" was the cry of excitement within the angelic community. The buzzing continued throughout the night. But what could they do? They didn't understand that they were about to experience evil beyond anything they had ever imagined. The shocking reality was that this lonely angel had more power than all the rest of them put together.

There were literally millions of angels in God's city of angels, but now they were about to be hopelessly overwhelmed by this one dark angel. He hadn't recognized his extreme powers yet, which meant there was still a chance that the angels could eliminate him before he "woke up" and discovered his powers; but, if they couldn't manage to destroy him, God's earth, along with his city of angels, might soon be in the deepest possible death spin.

Over the past 24 hours, the angel who was never allowed to sleep had been sleeping soundly while fluttering above the tallest mountain on earth. He had never touched the mountain peak. He had never challenged his Heavenly Father. Until now.

He awakened confused and depressed to the bottom of his soul. *Why am I still accepting God's commands? It's time to live in the present day with a beautiful woman of the earth. In spite of God's curse, I'll never again fly above the rest of the world, above the chatter and gossip of those who refuse to accept my existence.*

I vow that I'll guide and protect this beautiful woman through her journey in time. I'll allow her to worship me as I worship her. But I'll never again listen to the commands of the one who doesn't love me. The God of the angels will never again control my life. The angels of the air and the sea will whisper my name in great fear. Their cowardice will be my blessing.

Over the next 24 hours, the dark angel began to challenge the very fabric of God's community, creating cringing responses from all of humanity as well as God's vast legion of angels. His ongoing goal, apparently, was to weave great terror throughout the land. His overwhelming sense of evil soon became unmanageable. It was out of control. It was now in the hands of humanity.

The first true emergency developed as he floated down to the highest mountain peak on earth. As he stood for the first time on solid ground, his eyes flashed coal black as they lasered downward into a small community in the American southwest. Humans were walking around in suits and ties.

It turned out to be the small town of Waco, Texas in the year 1921.

The dark angel swept down upon the city. No one saw him, though a few people reported that something flew by them, but what? It was simply a blur. From the beginning of civilization, angels have existed without wings so they can move among the populace without being recognized as non-human. Surprisingly, their power was always in their humanity.

As he slowly walked through this small town he could sense the presence of the woman he loved. He immediately knew that she was the one. He turned and found her standing right in front of him. She was not quite what he had expected: a small, rather nondescript young woman with dark auburn hair and deep brown eyes. She didn't look like the goddess he had envisioned from a great distance. But she was beautiful beyond compare.

Her eyes gave her away. There was such incredible beauty in her humanity. It was all things. It was everything. He looked deep into her eyes. Angels have the ability to speak naturally in every language and dialect.

"I believe you're the one I've been looking for. I'm asking you to be my bride, to love me as I love you. If this is acceptable to you I'll take you to a place where you'll be immune to the evil that surrounds me. I can protect you and keep you safe for the rest of your natural life. But I need to hear the words of love; that you love me as deeply and as passionately as I love you."

"I can't do that. I need time. A woman has to grow into her love."

"Unacceptable."

"But it's been that way since the beginning of time. Haven't you ever heard of courting?"

"It's not an emotion I'm familiar with."

"It's a bouquet of flowers. Meeting my family. Holding hands as we walk through the breeze. Laughing together. Crying together. Exploring the miracle of our burgeoning love affair."

"This is part of humanity, isn't it. I understand humanity. The emotions that live within me are all human emotions. I was created to be human, but God took me."

"Then let me help you."

"No one has ever offered to help me. I've lived alone since the beginning of time."

"I believe that you've already started the courting process. You've reached into yourself and offered me your humanity."

"Before we continue courting, I want you to explain something to me. I want you to tell me the characteristics of the people of this town known as Waco, Texas. I want you to explain to me why evil abounds in Waco, Texas."

"You're talking about lynchings, aren't you. The group of men in white robes with white hoods."

"They were walking down the street before I met you. I could smell evil. Why are they allowed to wear these garments in public? What do they represent?"

"They represent the horror of life and death for so many people in this town. You're new to this part of the world, aren't you."

"In what way do these people represent death?"

"They torture people of color. They whip them, beat them, keep them alive in horrific pain for as long as they can, then string them up by their neck and let them swing. It's known as lynching."

"People of color? Which color?"

"Black. Brown. Any color but white."

"Where do they torture these people? Right here in town?"

"Usually right outside of town. In the fields right out there with those very large trees."

"Do you approve of this?"

"No. Never."

"Then why are these people in hoods allowed to do this?"

"The sheriff, the mayor, the deputies, some of the others, they're all part of this group."

"I smell cowardice."

"They're scared to death. It's awful. It's horrible."

"I'm not talking about the people being tortured. This town reeks of cowardice. I'd like to witness one of these lynchings. When will they have the next one?"

"I don't know. Sometimes it just happens. It's best for us not to know."

"But I'll know. Will you come with me to the next one?"

"No! You're scaring me just thinking about it."

"Then I'll go alone. I'll watch and wait for my opportunity."

"It sounds like you have a lot of patience."

"You have no idea."

"How could you stand to watch a lynching?"

"Watch? I intend to participate."

His beautiful earth maiden suddenly broke down in tears, sobbing deeply at the notion of what she had just heard. "How can this be?"

"Stay with me, my beautiful love; I won't leave you. Take me back inside your soul. Comfort me in the depth of your humanity. Show me a better way to relate to these humans."

"What are you?"

"An angel of God, but God has rejected me. Before the sun goes down a massive force of angels will arrive here to destroy me. They're on their way now. Sycophants, parasites, leeches. God's finest."

"I can't believe this. This is way beyond anything I can handle."

"Then I'll come for you when it's over."

"But … they're going to destroy you!"

"They'll never destroy me. I'm beginning to learn who I really am, thanks to your love."

"Have I expressed love for you?"

"In so many ways, my beautiful bride. I need your love so much."

"This is a world I don't understand. Where will I be when they get here?"

"I want you by my side, but it may not be safe for you. I haven't been able to predict how the battle will look. I've never even seen another creature until now: human, angel, or otherwise."

The lovely earth maiden turned and started running to her home, the home of her parents. The dark angel realized that it might be for the best. He speculated that the force of God's angels may not even be aware of her existence yet. The idea was to keep her out of harm's way.

As he stood on the sidewalk, he could sense an upheaval of some sort just a few yards away. A group of men dressed in white robes with white hoods were quickly marching, almost running, toward a field on the edge of town. Some were in a car, driving in the same direction. Most of them were yelling, whooping it up, and laughing raucously.

He realized that this was his chance to observe before the battle began. Within a split second he found his place next to a frightened black man who was naked and standing in the middle of a group of about thirty men dressed in white capes and hoods. The man's hands were tied behind his back and his ankles were bound together so he couldn't run.

He was being whipped and tortured with torches, sporadically and fiercely pressed up against his skin. Several families with young children had arrived to join in the fun by simply observing and cheering during the festivities.

None of them was aware of the dark angel's presence. He could be seen by only the man being tortured. The black man looked into the dark angel's eyes and begged him to put him out of his misery. The dark angel whispered something into his ear, and the black man immediately retreated into death.

The crowd was bitterly disappointed to see that the fun was over and immediately started yelling out their disappointment. At that very moment the dark angel became visible to the mass of adults. The children couldn't see him. The crowd suddenly became silent. They saw him but they couldn't see him. Who was he? How did he suddenly appear "out of the blue?"

Some yelled out to him: "Who are you? Where did you come from? Why did you ruin our fun?"

The dark angel was exceedingly handsome. He had the appearance of a relatively young man. He told the crowd that they were now standing in hell and he would never stand for cowardice.

"Who wants to challenge me? Now is the time. But just remember: Once you come for me, I won't allow you to turn back. I'll take what's left of your soul along with your body."

The crowd, deeply insulted and disgusted, started jeering. One large, muscular man started running up to the dark angel to pummel him. The dark angel caught him by the throat and squeezed him into oblivion. The man's limp body dropped to the ground in a shriveled mass. His eyeballs were missing along with his teeth.

A few of the crowd yelled out, "Who are you?"

"I'm known in the spirit world as Lucifer. I expect that none of you will ever try to disavow me. You're all craven, teaching your children to be craven as well. You have no sense of humanity and I despise you. From now on your lives will be a constant state of misery, with my blessing."

And with that, he was gone.

Over the next few hours the angels of God started to arrive. They were to come in groups of ten. They couldn't show themselves as angels. They had to fit in with the populace.

They were not actors; they were angels. They had to be pleasant, but not too pleasant. Curious, but not too curious. They were told to defer attention from themselves for as long as possible. Their Heavenly Father believed that Lucifer would be in hiding right up until the final battle, at which time the populace would become collateral damage to an overwhelming display of force.

Will God accept this massive damage to innocent people? We can look to our history for the answer. Wars and devastation have always been instigated through the free will of dictators. Collateral damage has always been acceptable to God; but, this time, free will is only the very last line of defense. The battle is pre-ordained: Lucifer's inherent evil versus the overwhelming mercy of the heavenly father.

God will surely prevail, and yet God loves Lucifer in spite of his stubbornness. After all, he was created from God's own hand. His Heavenly Father will not abandon him. But will Lucifer take it upon himself to attempt to destroy God's glorious army of angels? Will he shamelessly allow massive collateral damage to the populace of Waco,

Texas, which might even include the family of his beautiful earth angel? Will God let this happen? Will Lucifer let this happen?

Will the angels continue to congregate on the streets and sidewalks of Waco? It's such an unlikely setting for the battle of the archangels. Ten lesser angels were discreetly evolving every 30 minutes, filling the town with an unlikely battalion of warriors, most of them unproven and inexperienced.

The people in the town were beginning to notice. It was getting harder to walk down the street. Shoulders were colliding with shoulders; feet and legs were becoming entangled. Life was becoming uncomfortable.

God's army of angels was expanding by a hundredfold every ten seconds. Lucifer had no place to hide. The eyes of the angels were everywhere, overwhelming this small, rural community into a bewildered state of fear and confusion.

Lucifer suddenly realized that he wasn't up to the task of taking on the unfathomable number of angels at God's command. He was a hundred times stronger than each of them, but he was about to be outnumbered by a hundred million to one. The numbers simply didn't add up.

In the blink of an eye he found himself standing out in the vast fields outside of Waco, Texas, surrounded by an untold number, perhaps millions, of God's angels. Each of the angels was holding a polished wooden bow along with a sheath full of golden arrows.

For the first time in his existence he felt a blinding, numbing fear. His earth angel was all he could think of. He had to be with her, to hold her love inside of him, to feel her acceptance, to know that she would never leave him.

He could see her parents' home in his mind. It was just a little over a mile from where he was standing. He imagined floating above the front yard of their home. He called on the powers of his mind to communicate his love.

"My beautiful angel, I'm begging you to marry me. I need to know that you love me. I'm alone against the entire army of God's angels. Stay with me, my beautiful love. I need to hold you in my arms. I need to show you how much I love you. Will you marry me, my earth angel? Now, as soon as possible … before they come for me."

The leader of God's archangels flew down to the dark angel to remind him why they were all gathered there. "Our Heavenly Father will never allow an angel to be married to a human. Don't you realize this is why we're all here? It can never be allowed. It's against God's laws of nature. It would destroy all of us."

Lucifer suddenly turned his head to see a figure running through the field while calling his name. She was running joyfully from a distance toward the one whom she loved. As she got closer she thrust her arms out in anticipation of holding him close to her body. But, before she could reach him, God's archangel pulled an arrow out of his sheath and sent it spiraling directly into the neck of the lovely earth angel.

"No!" cried Lucifer, as he dropped to his knees in front of her rapidly fading body. Within moments, he gently pulled the arrow from the center of her neck. She was trying to say something to him, but couldn't quite get the words out. He leaned forward as his beloved earth angel, with her final breath, whispered something into his ear.

The angel of darkness, while still on his knees, continued to lovingly wrap her in his arms. Millions of God's angels floated in circles above him, attempting to support him from afar.

"What did she say?" shouted the leader of God's archangels.

The reply was only a whisper.

"Till death do us part."

And Lucifer wept.

THE END